the Windy Day

by

Tony Sandoval

CUB
HOUSE

I t was noon, and the wind was beginning
to blow. The porch floor was full of
toy soldiers. My brother said they
were marching toward a great battle,
and that's why he couldn't come fly
the new kite that I was making.

ut I was afraid to go alone, because the chickens were loose. And to get to the field where I could fly my new kite, I had to cross through the woods. And I always felt like there was something in there watching me, lurking in the shadows of the trees.

I was sure that these monsters were probably mean and looking to devour little girls, either cooked or raw, whichever their appetite felt like at the time.

That day, I was lucky. Nothing happened, although I'm sure that a lot of eyes were watching my every step. When I finally reached the clearing, the wind was strong and steady, absolutely perfect for my kite.

The sky was beautiful, with clouds of warm yellow and pink hues. My kite was flying happily among them. But a small dark cloud zoomed into this beautiful landscape at full speed . . . a pirate cloud!

The pirate cloud was piloted by very evil
goblins who loved to steal children's kites,
leaving them sad and in tears. Because
of course we know that goblins feast on pies
of misery and drink a tea made of tears.

They had many tricks up their sleeves:
they armed themselves with hooks
and harpoons in order to grab my
kite by the wing and capture it.

But this time, the goblins were not satisfied with just taking my kite. Oh, no. They slid down the rope to the ground to see what other mischief they could do.

As soon as they hit the ground, they snatched the kite from my hands and surrounded me! What would they do with me? I was scared!

Suddenly, a huge shadow emerged from the undergrowth. I was scared because it was so big and scary, but I couldn't run away! The goblins had me surrounded!

I t was a big animal, half-dog and half-wolf. It was so big that I felt like I was standing under a black, hairy tree. The wicked goblins were terrified and ran away as fast as they could!

As soon as the goblins had run out of sight, the big wolf-dog called to me. He explained that he was bored sitting in the woods alone, and he asked me if I wanted to play with him.

So I climbed on the back of the wolf-dog and he started running very, very fast! And my kite started to soar very, very high and very, very far!

After such an exciting race, the wolf-dog took me home. We crossed through the shadows of the forest, which weren't full of monsters after all! From now on, I wouldn't be afraid of them anymore . . . at least not any more than the chickens running free in my yard!

Since that day, the wolf-dog has been
my friend, and he makes me fearless.
So I nicknamed him "Courage"!

Translation, Layout, and Editing by Mike Kennedy

ISBN: 978-1-942367-98-7
Library of Congress Control Number: 2018962463

The Windy Day, published 2019 by The Lion Forge, LLC. Originally published in France under the title *Le Jour de Vent* © 2014 BELG prod Sàrl www.groupepaquet.net. All rights reserved. CUBHOUSE™, LION FORGE™ and all associated distinctive designs are trademarks of The Lion Forge, LLC. No similarity between any of the names, characters, persons, or institutions in this book with those of any living or dead person or institution is intended, and any such similarity which may exist is purely coincidental. Printed in China.

10 9 8 7 6 5 4 3 2 1